R0083735431

12/2015

 W9-BIP-911

Dear Dragon Goes to the Beach

by Margaret Hillert
Illustrated by Jack Pullan

NORWOOD HOUSE PRESS

DEAR CAREGIVER, The *Beginning-to-Read* series is a carefully written collection of classic readers you may remember from your own childhood. Each book features text comprised of common sight words to provide your child ample practice reading the words that appear most frequently in written text. The many additional details in the pictures enhance the story and offer the opportunity for you to help your child expand oral language and develop comprehension.

Begin by reading the story to your child, followed by letting him or her read familiar words and soon your child will be able to read the story independently. At each step of the way, be sure to praise your reader's efforts to build his or her confidence as an independent reader. Discuss the pictures and encourage your child to make connections between the story and his or her own life. At the end of the story, you will find reading activities and a word list that will help your child practice and strengthen beginning reading skills.

Above all, the most important part of the reading experience is to have fun and enjoy it!

Shannon Cannon

Shannon Cannon, Ph.D.
Literacy Consultant

Norwood House Press • P.O. Box 316598 • Chicago, Illinois 60631
For more information about Norwood House Press please visit our website at *www.norwoodhousepress.com* or call 866-565-2900.

Text copyright ©2016 by Margaret Hillert. Illustrations and cover design copyright ©2016 by Norwood House Press, Inc. All rights reserved. No part of this book may be reproduced or utilized in any form or by any means without written permission from the publisher.

LIBRARY OF CONGRESS CATALOGING-IN-PUBLICATION DATA
   Hillert, Margaret.
   Dear Dragon goes to the beach / by Margaret Hillert ; illustrated by Jack Pullan.
      pages cm. -- (A Beginning-to-read book)
   Summary: "A boy and his pet dragon take a family trip to the beach. Together they see sand, seashells, and the water for the first time. This title includes reading activities and a word list"-- Provided by publisher.
   ISBN 978-1-59953-704-7 (library edition : alk. paper) -- ISBN 978-1-60357-794-6 (ebook)
   [1. Beaches--Fiction. 2. Dragons--Fiction.] I. Pullan, Jack, illustrator. II. Title.
   PZ7.H558Debi 2015
   [E]--dc23
                2014043664

275N—062015
Manufactured in the United States of America in Stevens Point, Wisconsin.

The beach!
The beach!
Who wants to go to the beach?

I do! I do!
Dear Dragon and I want to go.

Let's go!
It will be fun.

Away we go.
Away we go to the beach.

Here we are at the beach!

Father, where is the beach?
I do not see water.
I do not see sand.

You will see.
We will walk to the beach.

This is the beach.
It is the sand next to the water.
We can play now.

Yes!
Here Spot.
Get this.

You did it.
You got it.
Good dog!

Look, Father!
I can make something in the sand.
Look what I made.

17

I can do this too!

Oh, oh.
The water makes it go away.

Mother, look what I have here.
One.
Two.
Three.

Here is a pretty one for you, Mother.

May I have something to eat?

Yes, this is for you.
Come and eat.

Oh this is so good.

But look at this!
This is not good.
Let's help clean this up.

I will get this.
You get that.
Let's put it all in here.

Here you are with me.
And here I am with you.
Oh what a fun day, Dear Dragon!

The following activities support the findings of the National Reading Panel that determined the most effective components for reading instruction are: Phonemic Awareness, Phonics, Vocabulary, Fluency, and Text Comprehension.

Phonemic Awareness: The /b/ sound

Sound Substitution: Say the words on the left to your child. Ask your child to repeat the word, changing the first sound to /**b**/:

kite = bite	felt = belt	get = bet	fun = bun
sand = band	make = bake	look = book	path = bath
goat = boat	turn = burn	mall = ball	day = bay

Phonics: The letter Bb

1. Demonstrate how to form the letters **B** and **b** for your child.

2. Have your child practice writing **B** and **b** at least three times each.

3. Ask your child to point to the words in the book that start with the letter **b**.

4. Write down the following words and ask your child to circle the letter **b** in each word:

beach	rub	garbage	build	ball
maybe	boy	bag	board	comb
boat	basket	umbrella	bucket	baby

Vocabulary: Compound Words

1. Explain to your child that sometimes two words can be put together to make a new word. These are called compound words. There are a lot of compound words that describe the beach.

2. Write down the following words on separate pieces of paper:

board	jelly	fish	week	sea	paddle
guard	boat	sand	castle	sun	glasses
walk	under	water	end	life	shell

3. What compound words can you create with the words above?

Fluency: Echo Reading

1. Reread the story to your child at least two more times while your child tracks the print by running a finger under the words as they are read. Ask your child to read the words he or she knows with you.

2. Reread the story, stopping after each sentence or page to allow your child to read (echo) what you have read. Repeat echo reading and let your child take the lead.

Text Comprehension: Discussion Time

1. Ask your child to retell the sequence of events in the story.

2. To check comprehension, ask your child the following questions:
   - Besides water, what does a beach have?
   - What are some things you should bring to the beach with you?
   - What can you make with sand?
   - What would you like to see and do if you go to the beach?

WORD LIST

Dear Dragon Goes to the Beach uses the 73 words listed below.
The **5** words bolded below serve as an introduction to new vocabulary, while the other 68 are pre-primer. You may wish to write the words on index cards and use them to help your child build automatic word recognition. Regular practice with these words will enhance your child's fluency in reading connected text.

a	day	I	play	walk
all	dear	in	pretty	want(s)
am	did	is	put	**water**
and	do	it		we
are	dog		**sand**	what
at	dragon	let's	see	where
away		look	so	who
	eat		something	will
be		made	spot	with
beach	father	make(s)		
but	for	may	that	yes
	fun	me	the	you
can		mother	this	
clean	get		three	
come	go	next	to	
	good	not	too	
	got	now	two	
	have	oh	up	
	help	one		
	here			

ABOUT THE AUTHOR Margaret Hillert has written over 80 books for children who are just learning to read. Her books have been translated into many different languages and over a million children throughout the world have read her books. She first started writing poetry as a child and has continued to write for children and adults throughout her life. A first grade teacher for 34 years, Margaret is now retired from teaching and lives in Michigan where she likes to write, take walks in the morning, and care for her three cats.

Photograph by Glenna Washburn

ABOUT THE ILLUSTRATOR A talented and creative illustrator, Jack Pullan, is a graduate of William Jewell College. He has also studied informally at Oxford University and the Kansas City Art Institute. He was mentored by the renowned watercolor artists, Jim Hamil and Bill Amend. Jack's work has graced the pages of many enjoyable children's books, various educational materials, cartoon strips, as well as many greeting cards. Jack currently resides in Kansas.